This edition first published in Great Britain 2000
First published in Great Britain 1994
by Egmont Books Ltd,
239 Kensington High St, London W8 6SA
Published in hardback by Heinemann Library,
a division of Reed Educational and Professional Publishing Ltd
by arrangement with Egmont Books Ltd.
Text copyright © Jamila Gavin 1994
Illustrations copyright © Kevin Hopgood 2000
The author and illustrator have asserted their moral rights
Paperback ISBN 1 4052 0133 9
Hardback ISBN 0 431 06181 5
10 9 8 7 6 5 4 3 2
A CIP catalogue record for this title is available from the British Library.
Printed and bound in the U.A.E.

DEADLY FRIEND

JAMILA GAVIN

ILLUSTRATED BY KEV HOPGOOD

 **YELLOW BANANAS**

To Heather, Louis and Rory

K.H.

The New Boy

'CHILDREN, MEET ADAM Starbright!'

The children gawped and giggled as their teacher frowned disapprovingly at their bad manners.

Adam Starbright stood stiffly at Mrs Walker's side. He was a bit like a dummy standing in the window of a clothing store. His face was as still as plastic and his eyes were the colour of water. His clothes were odd too. Mohun wondered where he had bought them. Not in Colston, that's for sure. You couldn't get anything worth wearing in Colston, except pants and vests and grannies' underwear. The clothes Adam Starbright was wearing were similar to the grey and maroon uniform they all wore, yet somehow different. They were smooth and tight fitting, as though his body had been poured into them.

Adam stared at Mohun. The new boy's eyes gazed steadily into his without blinking. Mohun stared back. He couldn't help it. It was as if Adam's gaze was a trap which had caught him and wouldn't let him go.

At that moment Gary Williams hissed across to Stephen Pitts, 'Adam Starbright! What a silly name. Do you think he goes twinkle twinkle in the dark!'

A ripple of sniggers swept around the room, as others repeated the joke.

Mohun, who still looked at Adam, heard the joke but didn't laugh. He remembered his own first day at school a year ago, when everyone had laughed at his name.

Although he had plenty of friends now, Mohun would always remember that day with a shudder. Adam didn't join in the laughter. He just gazed steadily at Mohun, as if he knew that Mohun too had been through the same experience and understood. They would be friends.

The sniggers rose louder, then stopped abruptly as Mrs Walker shouted above the hubbub.

'Children! Please!' Then she turned to Adam and said, 'I want you to sit over at that table between Mohun and Natasha. Go as quickly as possible.'

Adam went at once, in a straight line, across the tables, leaping on to the first and then striding across the tops to the next and the next until he arrived in his place.

'Well, REALLY!' exclaimed Mrs Walker breathlessly. 'What DO you think you're doing?'

'I calculated that the route I took to my desk was quickest by one point three and a half metres. Would you like me to show you my calculations?' asked Adam. 'You required me to go to my place as quickly as possible. So I did.'

'Adam! . . .' Mrs Walker began angrily. Then she stopped. He wasn't being insolent. He meant it. She paused, to give herself time to think, then she said, 'In future, NEVER on any account, step ON or OVER the tables. Tables are not for walking over. They are for sitting AT. Do you understand?'

'Yes, Mrs Walker,' replied the boy. 'I will not forget.'

'Now then, everybody, get out your English notebooks. I want you to write about your best friend.'

Mohun and Simon Boston grinned at each other across the room. They were best friends.

They would write about each other. There was
a rattle of drawers opening, as everyone pulled
out exercise books and snatched up pencils.
Out of the corner of his eye, Mohun had the
impression that Adam didn't open his drawer.
The boy's hand went straight through the table
top, as if it were water, and came out holding
his book. Mohun opened his mouth to exclaim,
but Adam caught his eye with a smile, slowly
twisting a pencil in his fingers. Then in a strange,

printy handwriting, moving to the right and back again to the left across the page like a computer printout, Adam wrote, 'My best friend is Mohun Banerjee.'

At break, Mohun, Simon and the others rushed out into the playground. Adam stood alone as the classroom emptied.

'Hurry out and play,' Mrs Walker urged him kindly as she collected up the exercise books. She nodded towards the playground, which they could see through the windows. Then she strode from the classroom, expecting Adam to follow. Out in the corridor, she turned to ask him whether he had brought a packed lunch, but he had vanished.

'Adam?' She looked back inside the classroom. There was no sign of him. 'Adam?'

Out in the playground, Adam raced towards Mohun and, with a flying leap, caught the football which Mohun had just kicked to Simon.

The Information Gatherers

'OH DEAR!' INFORMATION Gatherer 6 hissed
through his teeth. 'I forgot.'

'What did you forget?' asked Mater, leaning
over his shoulder and staring at the television
screen. IG6 had zoomed into a closeup of Adam
and Mohun side by side. Mater smiled with
satisfaction. She couldn't help feeling a sense
of pride at the way in which they had adapted
Adam to the planet Earth. You could hardly tell
that he was any different from the other children.

'I forgot to inform him about doors,' said IG6. 'He should have gone out through the door not through the wall. Humans have not yet learned how to break up into molecules. They still have to create spaces through which to pass, such as doorways and corridors.'

'That's the third error you've made today, IG6,' muttered Mater.

'Yes . . . yes . . . I'm not used to the slow speed with which they move on Earth.'

IG6 shook his head with wonder. 'But Adam has done well. He has carried out another task and now knows what a *school* is. He is following his instructions with credit.'

For two thousand years, the Information Gatherers had been exploring space. They had been searching for a planet with life on it.

Then they found Earth. Mater still shivered with the excitement of the discovery. Plans were made to send out research teams. How proud she was when her son, Adam, was chosen to join the team and gather information about life as a human child.

'Now he is investigating something called a *friend*. Do you think this human child is a *friend?*'

Mater and IG6 looked with interest as Adam kicked the ball to Simon.

The New Game

'ARE YOU COMING skateboarding after school?'
asked Simon.

'No . . . I . . . ' Mohun hesitated, struggling
briefly with himself.

'Go on!' urged Simon. 'I've got some new
tricks to show you!'

'Simon, I've reached level nineteen in my
new computer game. I must go on . . . don't
you see?' Mohun tried to explain, longing to
share his excitement with his best friend.

But Simon's voice was flat with disappointment. 'You never used to be like this,' he said.

'I've only got one more level to go and then I reach the Ultimate Destination and claim the prize.'

'What sort of prize?' asked Simon, slightly more interested.

'I don't know. It's a surprise.'

It had all started one day when the postman delivered a small brown packet to Mohun's house.

'It's for you,' Dad had said, tossing it to his son.

Mohun had ripped off the paper with excitement. Inside was a computer disc without a name. He rushed up to his room and slotted it in. Up on the screen came a title: 'Ultimate Destination'. A brief note told him that he had been selected to receive this computer game free, and that if he achieved the Ultimate Destination, he would get a fantastic prize.

The game was to help Information Gatherers from another planet who were travelling through space. They were collecting knowledge about star systems and sending it back to their base. Mohun had to blast away space pirates and dodge their way through rock storms; he had to rescue them from the magnetic pull of black holes and guide them from one planet to another, fighting off alien monsters and deadly microbes. At each step, he had to gather information and then move on to the next level of the game. It wasn't quite clear what or where the Ultimate Destination was. The instructions told him that he would know when he got there.

That was weeks ago, and ever since the disc arrived, Mohun had been playing it every spare moment. His mother got very upset with him.

'That game's taken over you,' she wailed. 'You don't care about anybody any more, not even Simon and he's your best friend! He used to be round here every day, now I haven't seen him for weeks. You don't eat, you don't sleep. You think of nothing but that machine. I feel like unplugging it!'

Mohun was horrified.

'Mum, don't. Don't ever touch my computer. It's taken me weeks to get to level eighteen. I've only another two levels to go and then I reach the Ultimate Destination. I'd die if you wiped the game or set me back to the beginning. Do you realise, I'd DIE'

Now he had reached level nineteen. Only one more level to go. The Information Gatherers had found a planet with life. A message appeared on the screen.

'MOHUN. DON'T GIVE UP. YOU ARE NEAR TO THE ULTIMATE DESTINATION.'

Virtual Reality

'YOU DID WELL today, Adam!' Mater appeared before him.

On the new housing estate at the bottom of the road, the Information Gatherers had created Adam a house in Virtual Reality; a house which was not real to anyone else except Adam. No one else could see it, because no one else had the special sensitive suit which covered his whole body like a skin.

They had created a house such as humans lived in. They wanted to understand everything about the human way of life. So Adam now sat on a comfy sofa watching television, with a plate of Marmite sandwiches at his side and a mug of hot chocolate in his hand.

'Mater!' protested Adam, as his mother appeared on the living room carpet, interrupting his TV

viewing. 'I'm watching cartoons. Everyone on this planet seems to like cartoons. I do too. They're fun!'

'Is this the boy with whom we have been playing Ultimate Destination?' The cartoons vanished and a picture of Mohun appeared on the screen. He was sitting in front of his computer in his room, furiously tapping the control pad.

'Yes,' said Adam, 'and this boy will be my friend.'

'*Friend*. We do not understand what a *friend* is,' frowned Mater.

The Information Gatherers had consulted the Space Dictionary. It said Friend: 'a person whom one knows well and is fond of.'

'Yes, a friend is another being with whom you like to be. But there is something more. *Fond*. What is *fond*? We don't understand that. We wish you to bring back this *friend* for further study. This information is of great importance and must be collected.'

'There is one problem,' said Adam. 'My friend already has a friend. He must be disposed of.'

Friend or not?

MOHUN STARED AT the computer screen. In this last level, the game had changed. Now, he wasn't just firing rockets and lasers at attacking alien forces, he was being asked to exterminate an enemy here on Earth. But first he had to identify the enemy by asking questions.

Mohun tapped away and soon constructed an indentikit on the screen. Excitedly, he built up a description. The boy was one metre, six centimetres tall; white-skinned with blue eyes and fair hair; hobbies: football and skateboarding . . .

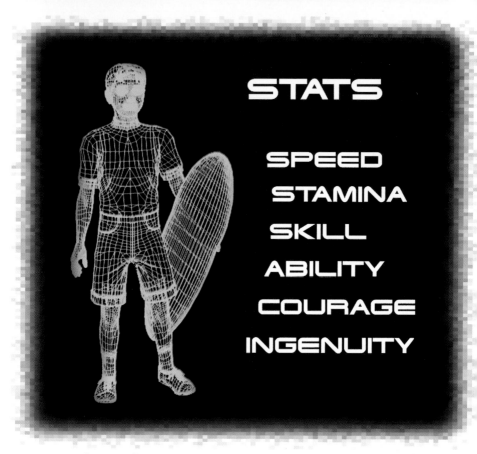

A figure began to appear. It was a boy, about his age. He was skateboarding with a large group of other boys.

Mohun felt uneasy. He knew it was only a game, but . . . this looked real. Instead of space monsters, was he being asked to exterminate humans? Slowly, he took up the control pad. Reluctantly his thumbs hovered over the trigger, ready to fire.

The camera zoomed in closer to one of the boys. He was moving fast on his skateboard. It tracked quickly to keep up with him. The boy twisted and whirled round. The boy reached a slope and hurtled down, spinning in the air and landing perfectly at the bottom. He turned and threw up his arms in a gesture of triumph.

The camera came right into close-up.

'THIS IS YOUR ENEMY,' said the words beneath the picture.

It was Simon.

Mohun's hand jerked with the shock as he fired automatically, then he fell away from the computer in horror.

'That was my friend,' he screamed. 'That was my friend.'

He stumbled out of the room and down the stairs. He was running now. Running for all he was worth. He raced towards the park. He ran without stopping until he reached the gates, then the paved area around the pavilion and the slope on which all the skateboarders liked to practise. A crowd of people stood in a tight cluster. No one was skateboarding; they were all looking down at someone.

'There's been an accident,' someone said. 'Blooming skateboarders. A right menace they are.'

Mohun pushed through to the front. 'Simon?' he shouted desperately. It wasn't Simon. Mohun felt relief sweeping through him. Another boy lay curled up on the ground. Simon bent over him with concern.

'What happened?' asked Mohun in a shaky voice.

'The skateboard just flipped under me!' whispered Simon. 'But I don't understand it. I had already stopped. Something seemed to strike my skateboard and make me crash into Kevin.'

'Simon, I'm sorry!' stammered Mohun.

'Why?' asked Simon, puzzled. 'How can it be your fault?'

An ambulance came. The ambulance men checked Kevin carefully.

'No damage done that I can see,' said one of them cheerfully, 'but we'll take him off for an X-ray just in case,' and Kevin was whisked away.

As the crowds dispersed, Mohun suddenly saw Adam Starbright. Was it the late afternoon sun which seemed to make his body shimmer? He was by a tree at a distance. His eyes gleamed like metal balls.

They looked at each other. Mohun heard Adam's voice in his head saying, 'It's a pity you missed.'

Mohun frowned. 'Missed what?'

'The enemy,' said Adam and smiled.

Mohun felt a strange chill come over him.

'You can leave it to me, if you like,' came Adam's voice. 'I wouldn't want you to fail getting to your Ultimate Destination.'

Mohun shuddered. 'I've got to go!'

'Where are you going?' cried Simon, trying to grab Mohun's arm. 'What about me!' But Mohun had gone.

The Deadly Game

AT HOME MOHUN stared at the screen. It was different. Now it was laid out like a maze. Standing at the top left-hand entrance to the maze was a menacing figure in red.

He was the Annihilator, with a deadly weapon in his hand. He waited for Mohun to take up the control pad and move him towards the target. The target was in the very middle of the maze. It was Simon!

Mohun stared desperately at the screen. Simon was skateboarding home; sometimes picking up his skateboard to walk over grass or to cross a road, but then jumping on to it again, when there was a clear hard space.

'Welcome back to the game, Mohun.' The words appeared on the screen.

Mohun sat down.

'Do you still wish to reach Ultimate Destination and claim your prize?' asked the computer.

For weeks Mohun's whole aim had been to get to Ultimate destination. Now everything had changed. He seemed to be playing a deadly game, in which the last obstacle to his success was Simon. Simon was the final target and unless he eliminated him, he would never gain the prize.

Before, every time the computer had asked him, 'Do you wish to reach Ultimate Destination?' Mohun had pressed 'Y' for Yes. But now as he stared fearfully at his friend, innocently skateboarding home, Mohun tapped 'N' for No.

Suddenly a purple figure appeared in the bottom right-hand corner of the screen. It was another Annihilator. Someone else was controlling it. It moved quickly through the maze getting nearer and nearer to Simon.

Mohun leapt to his feet, and ran to the door.
His first instinct was to warn Simon. Then he
stopped. The Purple Annihilator was moving
ever nearer. Mohun knew he would never
reach Simon in time, and even if he did, how
could they escape the Annihilator?

He returned to his chair. He tapped in a
message: 'I wish to play the game.'

He grabbed the control pad as the computer said, 'Play.'

He pressed the button. His Red Annihilator moved from its top left corner. Mohun had control again. As the Purple Annihilator advanced from the right, Mohun's thumb hammered away. He guided his Red Annihilator through the maze towards Simon.

Simon had reached the top of his road. He had the strangest feeling that he was being followed. He looked behind him. A purple figure turned the corner and was catching up with him. Ahead of him he saw another figure all in red, coming towards him.

Simon got off his skateboard. He felt afraid.

He didn't know why. He picked it up and
slowly crossed the road. Like a double shadow,
the figures crossed too and were still closing
in on him.

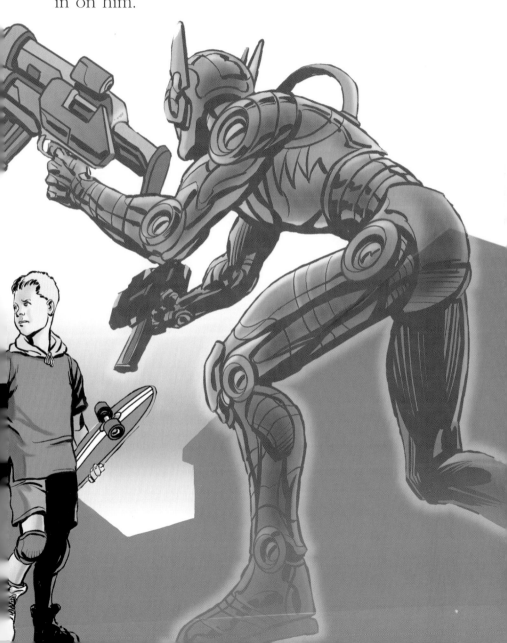

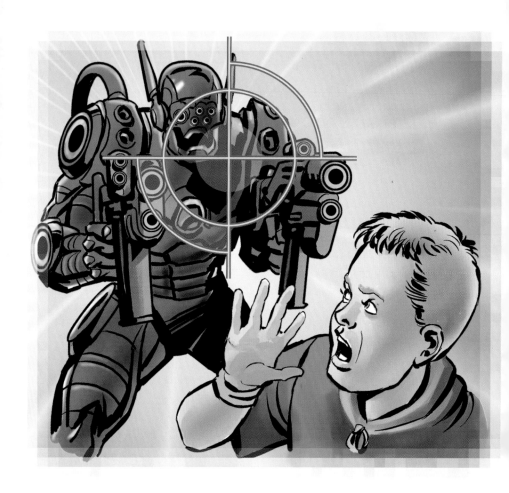

Mohun's thumb tensed over the button. His Red Annihilator was within range now. He stopped and waited. The Purple Annihilator continued getting closer and closer to the target; now he too was within range.

'Ready . . . aim . . .' Mohun's thumb trembled over the button of the control pad . . . 'FIRE.'

Mohun rammed his thumb down on the button. He aimed, not at Simon, but past him. He caused his killer to overshoot the target at the moment that both Annihilators fired.

The whole screen seemed to explode and then went blank.

Simon stood frozen to the spot in a state of shock. His skateboard lay in the gutter where it had rolled. Behind him Mohun was racing up the road. Before him stood Adam Starbright.

Mohun came and stood next to his friend. He put his arm around Simon's shoulders.

'Did you finish your game?' asked Simon.

'Yes.'

'What was the prize?'

'You,' said Mohun. 'Come on. Let's go.' Simon picked up the skateboard.

'Mohun!' Adam called out, His voice sounded crackly, like a radio wave. 'I only wanted you to be my friend.'

'You don't make friends by making enemies,' replied Mohun, and he and Simon turned away, walking side by side towards home.

Going Home

'THERE ARE THINGS about humans which we do not yet understand,' murmured IG6.

He and Mater studied the screen before them. 'We need more information. Our knowledge about humans is incomplete. We do not understand the meaning of *friend*.'

Mater looked it up in the dictionary again. "*Friend*: a person whom one knows well and is *fond* of,"' she read out loud.

'And what is *fond*?' asked IG6.

"*Fond*: having a liking for someone or something,"' read Mater. "'Tender and affectionate." We must instruct Adam.'

IG6 and Mater looked at the screen. Adam stood alone in the empty street.

'Bring him home,' Mater said.

Adam looked up into the sky. How lonely space was. The first evening star glimmered as his body melted and disintegrated into millions of molecules.

Yellow Bananas are brilliantly imaginative stories written by some of today's top writers. These beautifully illustrated books provide an excellent introduction to chapter books.

So if you've enjoyed this story, why not pick another from the bunch?

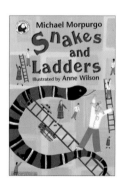